THE NOT-SO-ITSY-BITSY SPIDER

ALSO BY JOE McGEE

Junior Monster Scouts series

The Monster Squad

Crash! Bang! Boo!

It's Raining Bats and Frogs!

Monster of Disguise

Trash Heap of Terror

Night Frights series

The Haunted Mustache

The Lurking Lima Bean

NIGHT FRIGHTS

#3

THE NOT-SO-ITSY-BITSY SPIDER

BY **JOE McGEE**   ILLUSTRATED BY **TEO SKAFFA**

ALADDIN

New York London Toronto Sydney New Delhi

☙ALADDIN

An imprint of Simon & Schuster Children's Publishing Division
1230 Avenue of the Americas, New York, New York 10020
First Aladdin hardcover edition February 2022
Text copyright © 2022 by Joseph McGee
Illustrations copyright © 2022 by Teo Skaffa
Also available in an Aladdin paperback edition.
All rights reserved, including the right of reproduction in whole or in part in any form.
ALADDIN and related logo are registered trademarks of Simon & Schuster, Inc.
For information about special discounts for bulk purchases, please contact Simon & Schuster Special Sales at 1-866-506-1949 or business@simonandschuster.com.
The Simon & Schuster Speakers Bureau can bring authors to your live event. For more information or to book an event contact the Simon & Schuster Speakers Bureau at 1-866-248-3049 or visit our website at www.simonspeakers.com.
Designed by Tiara Iandiorio
The text of this book was set in Adobe Garamond Pro.
Manufactured in the United States of America 0122 FFG
10 9 8 7 6 5 4 3 2 1
Library of Congress Control Number 2021941922
ISBN 9781534480957 (hc)
ISBN 9781534480940 (pbk)
ISBN 9781534480964 (ebook)

For spiders everywhere—

especially Charlotte, Shelob, and all the

spiders in my house and yard

THE NOT-SO-ITSY-BITSY SPIDER

Greetings, my friends, and welcome to the curious, strange, and spooky town of Wolver Hollow—a town of shocking supernatural events and things that go bump in the night. I am the Keeper, your mysterious narrator and guide to the twisted tales that happen here. Make no mistake, my friends—this is a story so terrifying, so unbelievable, that you may want to think twice about turning this page. Oh, feeling bold, are you? Well, don't say you weren't warned. And now, for the first time ever, in writing, I present to you a story of two twins and a very large, very unexpected houseguest with eight long legs. You may want to read this one with the lights on!

1

Travis and Tara sat on the couch, noisily munching popcorn and watching the television. *Attack of the Space Lizards from Mars* was on, and no matter how many times they'd seen it (fourteen, to be exact), they always jumped when Captain Duke Ross opened the spaceship's supply closet and—

"AAAAAAAAAAHHHHHHHH!" they screamed. Popcorn flew everywhere as the twins just about leapt off the couch.

"Do you have to scream *every* time?" Mom asked. She pulled her coat on and grabbed her purse.

"And throw popcorn *every* time?" asked Dad.

"Don't worry," said Rachel, their babysitter. "I'll make sure they pick it up."

Tara and Travis rolled their eyes. They didn't think they needed a babysitter, not when they were in fifth grade. Babysitters were for babies, and they were *not* babies. Nevertheless, Mom and Dad insisted. Rachel had been babysitting them ever since they could remember. She was in high school and occasionally had cool stories, and she let them stay up later than Mom and Dad's instructed bedtime, and sometimes

she brought over a cool movie or a board game. So, as far as babysitters went, she wasn't half bad. But still . . . *babysitter*.

"Be good, kids," said Mom.

"We shouldn't be too late," Dad said.

"No problem, Mr. Booker," said Rachel.

Mom and Dad stepped out and shut the front door behind them.

"So," said Rachel, "who wants to play a game?"

But Tara and Travis weren't listening. They were on the edge of their seats, caught in the glow of the television. On the screen, Captain Duke Ross, galactic hero and the sole survivor of the Mars Expeditionary Force, crept down the darkened hallway. His footsteps echoed on the metal grating. Red emergency lights lit his way.

"*Only one way to save mankind,*" he said, looking into the camera. "*I'll have to trigger the ship's self-destruct button.*"

"That seems a bit drastic, doesn't it?" Rachel asked.

"Shhhhh!" said Travis and Tara at the same time.

"But . . . ," Rachel began. She sat down on the couch next to Tara and chewed her bubble gum entirely too loudly.

"They're on his ship!" said Travis.

"Who is?" Rachel asked. She blew a bubble.

"The space lizards from Mars!" said Travis.

"And he doesn't know where they are!" said Tara.

Rachel popped her bubble with a loud crack.

"Rachel!" Tara and Travis shouted.

 7

"Okay, okay," said Rachel. She stood up and adjusted her ponytail. "I'll be in the kitchen if you need me. I'm going to see what ice cream you have and call Marcy."

If Tara and Travis heard her, they didn't say anything. They were captivated by Captain Duke Ross.

So captivated that they didn't hear the knob of the front door turn.

They didn't hear the door creak open an inch.

Two inches.

Four inches.

The old hinges groaned when the door swung open almost all the way.

It was enough to finally get their attention.

"You guys are back early," said Tara.

"Yeah, what'd you forget?" asked Travis.

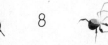

Their parents always forgot something every time they went out—Mom's purse, their keys, the pie they were supposed to bring to their card game. It was always something.

But when the twins looked back over the couch, their parents weren't standing at the entrance. No one was there.

Only the wide-open door, and the dark Wolver Hollow streets.

2

"They probably forgot to close it all the way when they left," Tara said.

"Yeah," said Travis. "The wind probably blew it open."

They stared out at the orange glow of the porch lights. A car drove down the street. Somewhere a cat screeched. But there was no wind. Not even a gentle breeze. Nothing that would have blown the door open. Yet there it was, wide open.

"We should probably close it," Travis said.

"Yeah, you should," said Tara.

"What do you mean *I* should?" Travis asked. "Why can't you go?"

"Because I got up last time, to get the popcorn."

"Why don't we both go?" asked Travis.

Tara shoved a handful of popcorn into her mouth and shrugged.

"Fine," said Travis, standing up from the couch. "Then you'll have to stay in here. All. By. Yourself."

Captain Duke Ross stood before the control room door, unaware of the shadow falling over him. Unaware of the creature that loomed behind him.

"If I can just unstick this lever . . . ," he said.
A clawed hand reached toward his shoulder from off-screen.

"Let's make this quick," Tara said.

The twins paused the movie and stepped into the foyer.

"There's no way this door opened on its own," Travis said.

"Well, someone opened it," said Tara.

Travis took a step forward.

"Hello?" he said. "Anyone out here?"

There was no answer.

"Hello? Anyone?" He nervously licked his lips. "This isn't funny."

Still nothing.

He leaned forward a bit more and then peered left and right, trying to see if someone was, indeed, hiding in the front bushes.

"Just close it and come in," said Tara. "It's probably nothing."

"Yeah," said Travis. "Probably nothing."

He closed the door and locked it, for good measure.

They were just about to turn around and head back to the den when a board creaked behind them. It was the loose hallway floor-board, the one that always made a sound if you put any weight on it. The twins had gotten in the natural habit of stepping over it whenever they walked down the hall.

They froze where they were.

"What was that?" Tara asked, refusing to turn around.

"The board," said Travis. Goose bumps crawled up his arm. "Someone stepped on it."

"Rachel?" Tara asked. "Is that you?"

No one answered. The foyer was deathly quiet. Tara and Travis stood still, eyes fixed on the front door. They were both afraid to look. There was no telling who might be standing behind them in the dark.

The board creaked again.

Someone, or something, had taken their weight off the noisy floorboard. But then they heard the breathing. Someone heaving in and out and in and out with a raspy, rattling breath.

Tara reached her free hand out ever so slowly, stretching her fingers toward the light switch.

The breathing stopped.

Tara flicked the foyer light on, and the twins spun around. Tara and Travis only caught a glimpse of something dashing through the opening that led into the dining room. Whatever it was, it was as big as a large dog, maybe bigger, and it definitely

had more than four legs. Travis grabbed
Tara's hand and squeezed. "Was that—"

"A spider?" Tara finished.

"AHHHHHHHH!" they both shrieked.

3

Travis reached the front door first. He unlocked it, yanked it open, and dashed outside.

Tara was right behind him. They didn't stop running until they reached the end of the driveway.

"I'm not imagining things, am I?" Tara asked. "That looked like a spider, right?"

"I only caught a glimpse of it, but I'm pretty

sure it was some kind of giant bug," Travis said. "It was fast, and hairy, and had more legs than I'm comfortable with! Whatever it was, it does *not* belong in our house!" The front door stood open, casting a long shadow on the steps. They watched the foyer for a few minutes, waiting to see if anything moved.

"What do we do, Travis? What do we do?" Tara hid behind the mailbox, ready to run for her life if anything besides Rachel appeared on the front step.

"We call the army," Travis said. "The National Guard. The house has to be destroyed. Maybe even the whole neighborhood, the whole town! We can't take any chances of it getting away."

"What about Rachel?" Tara whispered.

"It's probably too late."

"Travis!" Tara said, smacking his arm.

"What?" he said. "Let's assume it *was* a spider. . . . Did you see how fast that thing was? It's probably already got her. And why are you whispering, anyway? It's in there and we're out here, safe."

"I'm whispering because it might be listening to us," Tara said. "It might have good hearing or something. And we can't just leave Rachel in there, all alone with it, without knowing for sure if she's okay or not."

Travis groaned. "It's probably got fangs as long as my arm, dripping with poison. Or a stinger."

"Spiders don't have stingers."

"*If* it's a spider," Travis said.

"What does Dad always say?" Tara put on her best impression of Dad lecturing them. "'They're more afraid of you than you are of them.'"

"Well, Dad never saw a spider you could ride like a pony!"

"We'll just grab Rachel and get out," Tara said. "Leave the door open so that we have a quick getaway."

"If it doesn't pounce on us and eat us first," mumbled Travis.

"You do what you want," Tara said. "I'm going in."

Travis groaned. "Fine . . . but when we're eaten by whatever is in there, don't say I didn't warn you."

"Noted," Tara said. "Now come on."

They tiptoed up the walk and onto the front step and stopped. Nothing moved in the shadows farther down the hall. No heavy breathing or skittering footsteps. No scuttling

 21

or creaking. It was quiet—too quiet. The only sound was the sound of Rachel blabbing away on the phone in the kitchen.

"Rachel," Tara whispered as loud as she could. "Hey, Rachel!"

"It's no use," said Travis. "She can't hear us over her gossiping. Did she really just say she wants to ask Mark Dillman to go bowling?"

Tara rolled her eyes and grabbed her brother's elbow. "Let's cut through the living room."

Travis followed Tara, peering ahead, ready to bolt if anything should leap out at them. It was somewhere behind them, in the dining room. Or maybe it had already scurried into the study. Travis's head swiveled back and forth, watching, waiting.

Tara pulled Travis across the room, past

22

the glow of the television and the paused picture: a clawed arm reaching for Captain Duke Ross.

They both breathed a sigh of relief when they entered the kitchen. Rachel sat on the edge of the counter, twirling the long, curly phone cord with the receiver cradled between her shoulder and the side of her head.

"I know!" she giggled into the phone. "That's what I told her! I was like, 'Brad said that Anne said that Vicki said that if Michael asked Marcy to—hold on a sec.'"

Rachel pulled the phone away from her ear.

"What's up?" she asked. "Why do you two look like you've just seen a ghost?"

"There's a gigantic spider—" Travis started.

"We *think* it's a spider," said Tara.

 23

"But it's definitely big, and definitely hairy, and definitely wants to eat us."

"We *think*," said Tara.

"Well, what else would it want?" Travis asked. "Directions?"

Rachel rolled her eyes. "A spider? That's it? You're scared of a spider?"

"But it's—" said Tara.

"You know," Rachel said, "they're more afraid of you than you are of them."

Travis shook his head back and forth. "Not this one. It's . . ."

He held his arms out wide to demonstrate how big it was.

"It's in the dining room," Tara said. "We have to get out of here."

Rachel snorted and waved them off. "I think

you two have watched one too many scary movies. Hey, what would Captain Duke Ross say?"

"That we should press the self-destruct button and abandon ship," said Travis.

"Yeah, well, that's not happening," Rachel said. "Hey, I'm going to order a pizza in a minute. What toppings do you guys want?"

Tara and Travis just stared at her. Clearly she wasn't comprehending the severity of the situation. Right now, somewhere in their house, something huge, hairy, and creepy was waiting for them.

"Guys? Hello?" Rachel waved her hand in front of them. "Toppings? Okay, I'll just get pepperoni. And extra cheese."

She put the phone back to her ear and twirled the end of her ponytail.

"Hey, Marcy, I'm back. What? Oh, I don't know . . . something about a spider. Hey, let me call you back. I'm going to order a pizza. Be back in a sec."

Travis and Tara huddled by the refrigerator.

"Rachel might have had a point about Captain Duke Ross," Tara said.

"Like I said, the self-destruct button."

"No, Travis," said Tara. "What happened when Captain Duke Ross turned his flashlight on the space lizards from Mars?"

"Oh yeah," said Travis. "They ran away. They hated the light!"

"So maybe that's why it didn't run into the kitchen," Tara said. "Or why it didn't come back into the foyer after I turned on the lights. Maybe it doesn't like the brightness."

"What if we turn on all the lights?" Travis asked. "Maybe it'll leave."

Tara nodded and grabbed a rolling pin from the drawer. "But I'm not going anywhere without something to protect myself with."

Travis picked up a frying pan. "Good thinking."

They tiptoed toward the unlit dining room side by side. Tara held her rolling pin at the ready, and Travis was all set to swing his frying pan like a baseball bat.

The light switch was just inside the open doorway. All they had to do was reach to the right and flick it up.

Just reach one hand into the unseen.

Travis took a deep breath and then stretched

 27

his hand into the dining room, feeling around for the switch.

One inch.

Two inches.

Almost there.

And then a sharp, spiky claw moved across his hand.

"AHHHH!" Travis shrieked. He ripped his hand back out of the room. "Don't eat me!"

Tara screamed and leapt back, falling onto her behind on the kitchen floor.

There was a series of bangs and thuds from the study at the front of the house. Whatever it was, it was on the move! It must have run up and over Mom's piano, because the keys all crashed and jangled like something had pounded across them.

Travis held his shaking hand up, looking to make sure he hadn't been bitten. No marks, no punctures, but it had touched his hand!

"It tried to bite me!" Travis said. "It—it tried to eat me!"

"Did it get you?" Tara asked. "Are you poisoned?"

"No, no, I'm okay," Travis said. "That was close!"

The front door slammed shut.

Tara and Travis peeked down the hallway.

They had hoped it had left, but it hadn't.

It was worse. There was no longer any question as to what it was. It had to be a giant spider . . . and it had sealed the front door with thick strands of webs!

 29

4

"**What in the world are you two**

screaming ab—"

Rachel's question was suddenly cut off.

The twins spun back around to find the phone dangling from its cord and no sign of Rachel.

Marcy's voice continued to pour out of the receiver.

"Hello? Hey, Rachel . . . Rachel, cut it out. That isn't funny. Rachel?"

One long leg, as thick as a Wiffle ball bat and covered in coarse hairs, reached around the corner and pressed the button to hang up the phone.

Marcy's voice was replaced with a dial tone.

"It has Rachel," Tara said.

"It touched my *hand*," said Travis.

"It sealed the front door," said Tara. "We can't escape that way."

Travis nodded toward the side door at the end of the kitchen. It led out to the shed and the garage. But going out that way would mean that they'd have to pass the opening to the living room, the very place the spider was now, where it had reached out to disconnect the phone.

Click

The very place it had Rachel.

"We could get out that way if we're quick," he said. "Or through a window. After we save Rachel, that is."

Tara nodded. "After we save Rachel."

"We should call Marcy back, or the police," Travis whispered.

"But it's right there," Tara whispered back. "It's literally right on the other side of that wall."

"You reach for the phone, and I'll have my frying pan ready," said Travis. "As soon as I see just one leg, BAM! I smash it."

Two long legs with spiky claws

reached around the corner and ripped the phone from the wall.

"ACK!" Travis screamed.

"GAHHHH!" shrieked Tara.

The twins jumped back, practically falling over each other.

"There goes that plan," said Tara.

"Come on," said Travis, pulling his sister along. "It might not be hurt by the light, but it doesn't seem to like it, right? It keeps moving away from the rooms with the lights on, and it seems to be steering clear of the kitchen."

The twins turned on the lamps in the dining room, and then in the study. Books had been knocked from their shelves, chess pieces were scattered across the carpet, and a vase lay on its side. Sofa cushions were all flipped up

and out of whack as if something large had crawled underneath them.

"This is pointless," said Travis. "Every time we light up a room, it just runs away. We need a better plan."

"I bet that if we turn them all on, it'll run out of spaces to hide," said Tara.

The television in the living room started playing again, and the volume increased until the dramatic music of *Attack of the Space Lizards from Mars* was so loud that they could hardly hear each other.

"If there's one thing I know," said Captain Duke Ross from the small television, *"it's that no matter how dire things may seem, a true hero does not surrender to his fear. Stay back, lizard. You may be faster, stronger, and quite deadly,*

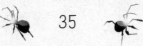

but . . . I am Captain Duke Ross." Laser blasts followed, and then the high-pitched, wounded cries of the space lizard.

"Easy for him to say," said Travis. "He has a laser blaster."

"What?" Tara asked.

"I said, EASY FOR HIM TO SAY. HE HAS A LASER BLASTER!"

Tara's eyes lit up.

Travis knew that look. That was the *I have a brilliant idea* look. It was also the look that often got them in trouble. But they were already in trouble. Dangerous and deadly trouble.

Tara pointed upstairs.

Travis nodded and followed her, tiptoeing toward the edge of the study and the foyer.

He wasn't sure what she was up to, but if she had something in mind, he might as well see what it was. Anything was better than their current situation.

Two unexpected things occurred next.

Rachel sat at the bottom of the stairs. A long silver web hung from the second-floor railing, attached to Rachel's web-bound wrists and ankles. A small glob covered her mouth. When she saw Tara and Travis, she tried to wriggle free, but it was no use. Before the twins could reach her, she was pulled straight up in the air and over the second-floor railing.

"Rachel?" Tara asked.

But there was no answer.

Then the doorbell rang.

5

"We're saved!" Travis shouted.

"Coming!" said Tara. "Hold on!"

DING-DONG! The bell rang again.

Tara grabbed the doorknob and pulled as hard as she could. But no matter how hard she tugged, the door wouldn't budge. The frame and hinges were stuck fast with crisscrossed lines of webbing.

DING-DONG! DING-DONG

DING-DONG DING-DONG!

"Hey, Rachel? It's Mark. Mark Dillman, from your math class? I . . . uh . . . I have your pizza."

"Mark, help!" Tara said. "The door is stuck!"

DING-DONG!

"Rachel, is that you?" asked Mark. "This isn't a prank, right? Because, um . . . I was hoping that maybe . . . you know, you might

want to go out sometime? Bowling, maybe?"

Travis rolled his eyes and pretended to stick his finger down his throat and gag.

"Mark! Mark, it's Tara and Travis!" Tara hollered over the maxed-out volume of the television set.

"He can't hear us," yelled Travis. "The TV is too loud!"

"Well, turn it down!" Tara shouted back.

"I can't find the remote," Travis hollered.

"Use the buttons on the TV!" Tara said, still tugging on the door.

"The TV has buttons?" Travis asked.

DING-DONGGGGGGGGGGGGGGGGGGGG!

"I totally understand if you're not interested," said Mark. "But your pizza's getting cold."

Travis found the volume controls on the television and turned it way down.

"Just a second!" Tara called back through the door. "The knob's stuck!"

"Okay, but I have, like, four more deliveries to make," said Mark. "My boss is going to be so mad if I don't deliver these pizzas soon."

Travis dashed to the window and threw back the curtain.

Mark Dillman stood on the front step in

his Pizza Mario uniform, complete with pepperoni-pizza-slice-shaped hat. Every few seconds, he would anxiously glance at his wristwatch.

As Travis watched, a wad of webs hit the pizza box with a loud *thwack* and snatched it right out of Mark's hands.

Mark looked up toward the second-floor windows. A second ball of sticky strands struck Mark, and he was yanked up off his feet and out of sight.

"HELLLPPPPPPP!" he cried, but half a second later his cries were muffled.

"He's gone," said Travis.

"What do you mean, 'he's gone'?" Tara asked. "He was just standing on the front step, trying to get Rachel to go bowling with him. If you help me get this door open—"

"I mean that he's gone from the step," Travis said. "Webbed and whipped up out of sight. The spider got him. Pizza too."

Tara stopped struggling with the knob.

"So, the spider has Rachel, Mark Dillman, *and* our pizza?"

"Yes," said Travis. "Somewhere up there." He pointed up the staircase to the second floor.

From the upstairs landing, something clicked and chittered. Tara and Travis lis-

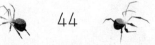

tened as a whole bunch of legs scampered away from the top of the stairwell.

"Great!" Tara said. "That's where our Super Sprayers are."

"You want to have a water-gun fight?" asked Travis.

"No—well, yes. I got the idea when you mentioned Captain Duke Ross's laser blaster."

"What idea, Tara?" Travis asked. "You're losing me."

"Haven't you ever heard that old nursery rhyme, 'The Itsy-Bitsy Spider'?" Tara wiggled her fingers through the air.

"Don't do that!" Travis said. "It creeps me out."

"'Down came the rain and washed the spider out'?"

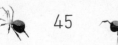

45

Tara glanced up the stairs to make sure it wasn't lowering itself down while they weren't watching. She shuddered at the thought.

"Yeah, well, I'm pretty sure that unless we have a fire hose, spraying it with water is *not* going to 'wash the spider out,'" Travis said. "This is too dangerous. I thought you had an actual plan."

"Maybe there's something else we can fill them with," said Tara.

"Like what? Lemonade? Quench its thirst? We have to get out of here, Tara."

"And leave Rachel *and* Mark Dillman? That's not what any true member of the Mars Expeditionary Force would do."

Tara knew his weak spot. There was no way he could back down from a mission when it

46

might be something that the Mars Expeditionary Force would undertake.

"Well, whatever we're going to do, we'd better do it fast," said Travis. "I'm not sure how far that pizza is going to go, and after that, it has two meal choices."

Tara's stomach did a somersault. "Gross," she said.

"You get the living room light," Travis said. "Let's not give it any more hiding options on the first floor. I need to check something real fast." While Tara took care of the only other first-floor room they hadn't had a chance to illuminate, Travis scanned the bookshelves in the study.

Mom and Dad were big readers. Maybe they had a book about . . .

"Aha!" Travis exclaimed.

He pulled a small, thick book from the shelf. *Natural Solutions for Unwelcome Intrusions* by Winston Oates. The front cover had an illustration of a line of ants marching across a kitchen countertop.

"Do I need to remind you that at this very moment, Rachel and Mark Dillman are in serious danger?" Tara asked. "You might want to hurry up."

"Okay, okay," Travis said. He scanned the table of contents and then stopped when he found what he was looking for. He flipped to page 294 and read. "Here we go. According to the book, spiders are repelled by strong, natural scents like white vinegar and peppermint oil."

Tara bit her lip and thought for a second.

"Mom uses white vinegar for cooking!" she said.

"What about the peppermint?" Travis asked, tossing the book aside.

"Not sure," Tara said. "But we'd better get up there on the double and get those water guns."

6

Tara turned on the staircase lights and then took a second to listen. She didn't want to rush into any trap the spider might have set, but she also did not want to waste any more time. Every second that ticked off the clock was one more second that Rachel and Mark Dillman were in danger.

When she was convinced that the spider

was not waiting above to pounce on her, she started up the steps.

She hadn't heard any clicking or scuttling. No heavy breathing. No eight-legged movement at all. And that was what terrified her. It was up there. But where?

Travis was right behind her.

"Hear anything?" he whispered.

"No."

"See anything?"

"No."

"What about smell?" Travis asked. "Smell anything funky?"

"No, shhh. Stop talking."

Tara reached the first landing and stopped. The stairs took a turn here and continued up

51

to the second floor. The steps might have been illuminated, but the upstairs hallway was not.

Tara turned to Travis and put her finger to her lips. Travis nodded.

One foot in front of the other, Tara told herself. Captain Duke Ross's words came back to her: *A true hero does not surrender to his fear.*

She stopped at the top of the stairs. Their bedrooms were right across the hallway from them, and each door was open, allowing the bright moon to shine in through the bedroom windows.

Bits of thick cobwebs stretched from the railing to the ceiling, and more sticky lines crisscrossed parts of the hallway. But there was no sign of what had made them.

It was eerily quiet.

Tara pointed to the light switch on the far wall. She was going to make a run for it. She held up one finger, two fingers, three fingers, and then she ran across the hallway, ducking under and dodging cobwebs, and turned on the hallway lights.

Nothing moved. Nothing jumped out at her or pounced on her. Nothing dashed out of the cobwebs to grab her and carry her off. But it was waiting somewhere—she knew it. And the minute they let their guard down, it would grab them with its eight hairy legs and spin them up like Rachel and Mark Dillman. They'd be just another snack.

She waved Travis forward, and he joined her outside their bedrooms. Tara's room was to their right and Travis's to their left.

"We stick together," he said, "and hope your water-blaster plan works. Where do you keep yours?"

"Closet. Where's yours?"

"Under my bed," he said.

"Let's get yours first," Tara said.

Travis shuffled over a few inches and slowly poked his head into his room. Spiderwebs covered his piles of clothes, his shelf of soccer trophies, and even his desk full of *Duke Ross: Explorer of Mars* comic books.

"Not my comic books," he moaned.

The window was open. That must have been where the spider had webbed Mark Dillman from, Travis thought.

Tara nudged Travis's elbow.

"Is it in there?" Tara whispered.

 54

"No, we're good," he said. "Check behind the door. I'll look under the bed."

Tara nudged the door closed with her foot, ready to dive out of the way if the monster was perched there. But it wasn't. Just Travis's poster of his favorite soccer player, Cameron Lucella.

Travis knelt in front of his bed. He was not about to just blindly reach underneath, not without looking first. That also meant that he might be putting his face right in front of the spider's fangs.

"Hurry up," Tara said.

Travis gripped the bed, thought of Captain Duke Ross and the Mars Expeditionary Force, and then quickly peered under. Nothing.

He grabbed his Super Spray Water Blaster and hurried to his feet.

 55

They did the same thing in Tara's room, moving quickly and with purpose. Quick check, grab the water blaster, and go. Time was of the essence, and they had no idea where their hunter was.

"Let's get that vinegar," said Tara. "Otherwise, like you said, these water blasters are useless."

"And then the hunter becomes the hunted," Travis said.

The twins stood at the top of the stairs,

water blasters in hand. Suddenly, all the lights went out.

The hallway, their bedrooms, even the foyer light that had brightened the bottom of the stairs. All dark.

Travis jogged back to the hallway light switch and flipped it up and down a dozen times.

"Nothing," he said.

"Power must be out," Tara said.

"But how?" Travis asked. "Do you think that it . . . that it had something to do with it?"

"I have no idea," Tara said. "But it knew to seal the front door. It knew to take the phone off the wall. Travis, in case you hadn't noticed, size aside, we are *not* dealing with just any spider. This spider is smart. Too smart."

Shadows seemed to move and shift in the

57

moonlight, and every shape suddenly started to look like it had eight legs.

"This is bad," Travis said.

"I know."

"I'm freaking out," said Travis.

"Me too."

"Well, if it did cut the power, it would have had to turn off the breaker, right?" Travis asked. "In the basement?"

Tara shrugged. "Maybe? Or maybe there's more. Maybe the whole town is overrun by abnormally large arachnids and they've shut down the entire power grid."

Travis shuddered at the thought.

"I'm going to pretend you didn't say that," he said. "One ginormous, bloodsucking web spinner is enough. I don't even want to think

about Wolver Hollow crawling with them."

"Okay, so then we're assuming it went down into the basement and turned off the breaker?"

"But we would have seen it, right?" Travis asked. "We were standing right here in the hallway. It would have had to pass us."

Tara was about to answer when something banged farther down the hall—an echoing sound of something thumping against metal.

"The laundry chute!" Tara said. "It's on its way back up!"

"We don't have the vinegar yet!" Travis said. "These things are useless!" He held his water blaster up.

"Come on, we can't let it out!"

Tara and Travis sprinted down the hall toward the linen closet. The laundry chute was a hinged

 59

flap in the wall with a heavy-duty child safety lock on it. Mom and Dad had installed it when the twins were younger and discovered that they could drop things, like eggs, from the second floor to the basement. The linen closet was open, and hurried steps banged against the sides of the laundry chute, drawing closer. Tara reached out and snapped the latch closed just as something pushed against the flap. A raspy hissing sound of frustration came from the other side as it slammed and beat at the hatch, but the handle held. After a few seconds, the spider stopped.

Before either of them could say anything, the footsteps hustled back down the chute toward the basement.

"It's going to try the basement!" Travis said.

"We've got to block that door!" said Tara.

The twins rushed downstairs into the dark foyer. They ran as fast as they could down the hallway and burst into the kitchen just as the basement door opened a crack and one clawed spider leg began to emerge.

Travis gave the door his best soccer kick.

"EEEEEEEEEEEEEEEEEEEEEEEEEE!"
shrieked the spider. It pulled its leg back, and
the door slammed shut.

Travis put his back to the door and pushed,
trying to keep it from opening as the spider
thumped and banged against it.

"Grab a chair or something!" Travis said.

Tara pulled a dining room chair into the
kitchen and wedged it under the doorknob.

The spider gave it one or two more good
tries, and then the attacks stopped. Travis and
Tara were breathing hard, but not so loud that
they couldn't hear the basement steps groan-
ing under the weight of the heavy creature.

"It'll probably go back up the laundry chute,"
Tara said. "I'm not sure how strong that latch is."

"And now it's mad," Travis said. "I think I

hurt it when I kicked the door shut."

"Well, now is our chance to find Rachel and Mark Dillman," said Tara. "While we know where the spider is. But we still need to be ready. Just in case it gets out before we find them."

Tara found a flashlight in the counter drawer. Then she pulled the pantry door open and found the vinegar.

"Wait until it gets eight eyes full of this," she said, pouring the vinegar into her water blaster. "It's going to wish it never came to *our* house!"

Travis grinned and filled his blaster up with vinegar.

"Ready?" he asked.

"Ready," said Tara.

DING-DONG!

The doorbell rang again.

 63

7

DINGGG-DONG!

Tara looked at Travis. Travis looked at Tara and shrugged.

"Maybe Mr. Gygax next door saw all our power go out and wants to make sure we're okay," he said.

"Or maybe it's the spider," Tara said. "Trying to trick us. We'll open the door and SPLAZZAP . . . we get webbed right up."

"It's in the basement, remember?" said Travis.

"How do we know that?" Tara asked.

"There are windows in the basement."

They crept down the hallway with their vinegar-filled Super Spray Water Blasters. Tara shone the flashlight in front of them, above them, and all around them. As they drew closer to the front door, the unmistakable red-and-blue flashing lights of Wolver Hollow's one and only police car became visible through the narrow side windows.

DINGGGGGGGGGGGG-DONG!

This was followed by a long and heavy knock.

"Anyone home? Hello?"

"It's Sheriff Macklin!" Tara said.

Travis tugged at the door again. "It won't budge."

"Stand back," said Tara. She aimed her blaster at the cobwebs and let them have it. It worked! The vinegar ate through the webs around the hinges and the frame.

Travis pinched his nose. "Ugh. I can see how it would chase spiders away. That stuff is potent!"

"Well?" Tara asked. "Are you going to open it or what?"

Travis pulled the door open just as Sheriff Macklin was about to rap on it again.

"Oh, hey, Travis, Tara," said Sheriff Macklin. He pulled his mirrored sunglasses down until they perched at the end of his nose. He looked over and past the twins. "Everything okay in here? I had a report of an"—he looked down at his notepad—"extremely loud television set playing.

66

Which, given the looks of things, doesn't seem right. Power out?"

Travis opened his mouth to say that things certainly were *not* right, that things were *not* okay, and that a creature out of his nightmares had their babysitter and Mark Dillman and was loose somewhere in the house, presumably in the basement. But nothing came out of his mouth because at that very moment a ball of silvery webs was being slowly lowered behind the sheriff. The creature wasn't in the basement—it had somehow gotten out and was upstairs!

The ball spun in a circle behind Sheriff Macklin. A message had been woven across the surface of it. It read:

I HAS RACHEL.

 67

"Y'all order a pizza?" Sheriff Macklin asked, turning to point back at the still-running station wagon with the Pizza Mario delivery cone fixed to the top.

Just as he turned around, the cobweb message was yanked back up out of sight.

"Shouldn't leave the car running like that," said Sheriff Macklin. "Bad for the environment." He tapped his pen on his notepad and pointed at Tara and Travis. "Climate change. It's real, you know."

The twins were speechless. They just stared past Sheriff Macklin.

"Now, like I was saying, loud television, something about a ruckus. Y'all having a ruckus? Doesn't seem like a ruckus. Seems like a slumber party. I'll bet you're having a

 69

slumber party, aren't you? Boy, I miss slumber parties. When I was a kid, we had slumber parties all the time."

Tara and Travis didn't say a word. They watched, wide-eyed, as another message was lowered down. It read:

SHHHHHHH . . . OR ELSE.

"I'll tell you what," said Sheriff Macklin. "I'm going to go turn that car off. You two stay right here. I want to hear all about your slumber party. Help me remember the good old days! You're not too old for slumber parties, right?"

Right before he turned around, the webbing was pulled back up out of sight.

"What the heck are we supposed to do?" Tara whispered.

"We have to tell him," Travis whispered back.

Sheriff Macklin walked back down to the pizza delivery station wagon.

The message dropped back down.

NO U DON'T, read the newly spun message. The message turned in a lazy circle. A second message had been woven on the other side:

I MEEN IT. I HAS POIZON.

"This is crazy, Travis," said Tara. "What kind of spider can write?"

"The kind that has taken complete control of our house and is holding two teenagers hostage," said Travis.

Sheriff Macklin turned the station wagon off. The webs disappeared from sight before Sheriff Macklin turned back toward the house.

"So where were we?" he said, stepping

 71

back up onto the porch. "Oh yeah, the party. Y'all are having a party. Hey, are your parents home? Mind if I say hello? Your dad still bowl? I keep meaning to join the league again. Maybe he has room on his team? Is he on a team? I mean, if he's not, we could always start a new team."

A new message appeared:

MAKE HIM GO AWAY.

"He's not home, Sheriff," Tara said.

"Yeah, um, they're out," said Travis. "Rachel is watching over things while they're . . . *hanging* out with friends."

"But it was nice of you to *drop* in," Tara said, quickly catching on to what Travis was trying to do.

"But don't let us keep you from your work,"

Travis said. "Wouldn't want you to fall *behind*." He nodded his head in the direction of the front yard, trying to clue Sheriff Macklin in.

Sheriff Macklin chewed on the end of his pen for a moment.

"I feel like y'all are trying to tell me something, but I'm going to be honest—I have no idea what it is. Probably some kind of kid code, huh? All right, well, you go on and get back in there and be good for Rachel. Keep that television turned down, and don't forget to tell your dad about the bowling team. Tell him I'll be thinking about a team name. Boy, that's exciting! Okay now, y'all be good."

The spider yanked its web up right before the sheriff turned around.

As soon as Sheriff Macklin's back was

turned and he walked to his patrol car, one last note dangled before them:

NICE TRY.

Sheriff Macklin waved and pulled away, leaving Tara and Travis standing in the open doorway, vinegar-filled Super Spray Water Blasters in hand.

8

They stood there for a minute, debating whether or not to run for help, or just simply run for their lives. But in the end, they didn't choose either of those things.

Travis closed the door and locked it. "We can't leave Rachel."

"Or Mark Dillman," said Tara. "You read that sign. It has *poison*. How long before it decides to start snacking on them?" She shivered at the thought of that spider sinking its sharp, poison-dripping fangs into Rachel or Mark.

"We need to find it, and find it soon," said Travis. "We've wasted enough time already. Sooner or later it's going to get hungry."

"Let's hope it's later," Tara said.

"We need to figure out where it's keeping them," said Travis. "It may be able to squeeze down the laundry chute, but they can't. So they're probably not being held in the basement."

"And we've been all throughout this floor," Tara said, motioning to the living room and study.

"It's gotta be upstairs, right?" Travis said. "Or in the attic. That's all that's left."

"But while we're trying to find and save

them, the spider is hunting us. It's fast, it's sneaky, and every time we think we know where it is, it's somewhere else. So how do we track this thing?"

Tara thought for a moment. Travis did too. Then it dawned on him. Tara's whole water-blaster idea had come from Captain Duke Ross and *Attack of the Space Lizards from Mars*. Captain Duke Ross had faced a similar situation on his spaceship.

"Do you remember when Captain Duke Ross had no idea where the last space lizard was?" asked Travis.

Tara grinned.

"Oh yeah!" she said. "He used his thermal sensor to look for the heat signature of the lizard's footprints!"

 77

"We might not have thermal sensors, but we can probably put something on the ground so that we can track where it's at, or where it's going," Travis said.

The pungent smell of the vinegar reminded Tara of her recent search through the pantry, and that reminded her of something that just might work.

"Flour!" she said. "There was a whole bag of flour in the pantry. We could sprinkle that on the floor upstairs."

Tara held the flashlight while Travis hefted the bag of flour out of the pantry. His water blaster was slung over his shoulder.

They climbed the stairs again with Tara in the lead. She had one hand ready to spray vinegar at anything that moved, and the flashlight in the

other. The beam of light scanned the walls, the floor, the ceiling. Her heart raced at the thought that at any moment she might catch sight of the giant spider in the shadows, ready to rush out and bite her. It was fast, very fast. They'd seen how quickly it had moved down the hallway, or from room to room, or even up the stairs, pulling Rachel along with it. Fast and strong.

However, her light did not reveal the spider, just strands of webs from where it had been.

"I don't see any movement," she whispered over her shoulder to Travis. "Just watch that you don't get stuck on any of these cobwebs. Let's start by pouring some flour over here." She gestured to the hallway to their left, where Travis's bedroom was and where the hallway turned and led to their parents' room.

 79

Travis shook flour out of the bag, sprinkling a decent amount on the floor.

"That should do it," he said. "Still half a bag left."

Tara crept forward, keeping the flashlight moving. Every so often, she would shine it behind them to make sure they weren't being stalked.

They passed Tara's room and the attic door, then stopped outside the bathroom. The door was slightly ajar. The spider could be in there right now, ready to spring.

Tara took another step forward and listened for any movement, or for that raspy breathing she'd heard before. Her palms were slick with sweat, and she could feel her heartbeat in her throat.

She handed the flashlight to Travis. He set the flour down and kept the light aimed straight ahead.

He nodded to Tara.

Tara nodded back.

She gripped the Super Spray Water Blaster extra tight, moved closer, and kicked the door the rest of the way open.

Something dark flew toward her. It rushed past her, brushing her ear in the process.

She screamed and jumped back into Travis, knocking the flashlight out of his hands.

It rolled in a circle, sending eerie shadows dancing along the walls.

But nothing had grabbed her, or bitten her, or wrapped her up. And when Travis finally recovered the flashlight and shone it back down the hallway, he discovered the source of the fright.

"It's just a bat," Travis laughed.

"A bat?" Tara answered. "You've got to be kidding."

A small brown bat fluttered in circles, knocking against the ceiling and the wall in a frightened attempt to escape.

"How'd a bat get into the house?" Tara asked, blowing a stray lock of tangled hair out of her eyes.

Travis pushed the bathroom door open and peered inside.

"Bathroom window isn't closed."

"Great," Tara said. "Spiders and bats."

The bat swooped toward them, right over their heads, and out the open bathroom window.

 82

"Well, there's one problem solved," Travis said. "Hold on, I'm going to shut the window." His eyes fell on the toothpaste tube sitting on the sink. Why hadn't he thought of it before? "Tara, look!" he said, holding up the tube. "Pepper—"

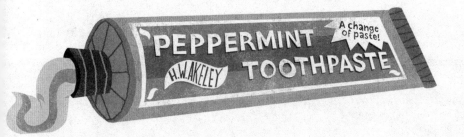

And just then, the shower curtain exploded outward, pulling rings off the shower rod and flying toward Travis. A big, dark shape on the other side of the curtain slammed Travis in his chest. He hit the floor with a loud thud, and the flashlight and

 83

toothpaste tube flew out of his hands.

"SPIDER!" Travis screamed. "Spider! It's on me! Get it off! Get it off, Tara!"

Tara spun toward Travis, squeezing her water-blaster trigger as fast as she could, spraying the bathroom, the hallway, the spot where she'd seen her brother go down. The shower-curtain-covered spider leapt from Travis's

chest and rushed by Tara. She shrieked and threw herself back against the wall.

Travis rolled to his stomach, grabbed the flashlight, and shone it down the hall. All he could see was the outline of something huge under the curtain as it careened into the wall and then disappeared around the corner.

Tara rushed to Travis.

"Are you okay? Did it bite you?"

"No," said Travis, half out of breath and jumping to his feet. "But come on! We've got it on the run!"

Travis ran after it, with Tara right behind him.

9

"Travis, wait!" Tara called.

But Travis did not wait. He ran.

When he rounded the corner where the spider had gone, it was nowhere to be seen. The shower curtain was there, but not what was under it only moments ago. However, the flour had worked. Every spot where one of its many legs had thumped along the floor was clearly marked by disturbed sections of flour.

It had run straight down the hall and into their parents' bedroom.

Travis stopped. He wasn't about to walk into a trap. They had it cornered. This was it. There was nowhere else for it to go.

"On three," Travis said. "One . . . two . . . three!"

He jumped through the doorway, swinging the flashlight left to right. He held his Super Spray blaster in his other hand. Tara was right behind him, vinegar blaster ready to fire.

Nothing.

He was breathing hard, his pulse racing. He couldn't watch every direction at once.

Tara stood shoulder to shoulder with her brother. "Maybe we should have turned the breaker back on."

"Too late now," said Travis. "Anyway, look."

He nodded toward a section of the carpet currently caught in the light's beam. More flour. The tracks led right to the slightly open closet door and stopped.

"This is it," Travis said.

"The final showdown," Tara said.

They moved closer to the closet door. Travis wiped a bead of sweat from his brow. Tara was breathing so hard, she thought she was going to pass out. They were about to come face-to-face with the biggest spider they'd ever seen in their life. Travis gripped the door handle.

And then it dawned on Tara. This was almost exactly the same scene that they'd paused earlier that evening, when they'd been watching the movie and thought their parents

 89

had come back for something. In that scene, Captain Duke Ross was reaching to open the last unexplored section of the ship, the ship's control room. But the last space lizard wasn't actually in there. It was a trick. The space lizard was behind him, and when they'd paused the movie, that webbed, clawed hand had been reaching right over Captain Duke Ross's shoulder.

Travis tightened his grip. Tara stared at the footprints. They stopped just outside the closet door.

Travis

began to pull

the door the rest of the

way open.

Tara turned her eyes toward the bedroom

ceiling and froze.

Staring back down at her were eight red eyes.

10

The spider clung to the ceiling, all eight legs spread wide and bent, ready to leap. Its body was covered in dark brown hair and coarse bristles. Two sharp fangs clicked together. It was easily the size of a large dog, or a small pony, or the goats they'd seen at Hennigan's farm.

"Travis, it's—"

The spider sprang from the ceiling and

landed on Travis's back, pinning him to the ground. Tara pumped the Super Sprayer and squirted the ceiling with vinegar just as the spider leapt. Before Tara could refocus her aim, it launched itself from Travis's back onto the wall and then back to the carpet, scuttling past Tara.

 93

Tara whipped around to let the spider have it, but it shot a thick strand of webbing right past her. The webs hit Travis in the side. The spider pulled, and Travis came hurtling forward, knocking Tara off her feet.

It quickly wrapped up Travis's ankles, spinning and rolling the silky threads with the sharp ends of its long legs. Then it took off down the hallway, pulling him along.

"Help!" Travis called. "HELP!"

Tara hopped to her feet.

But by the time she reached the hallway, both the spider and Travis were gone.

Tara was alone. *Almost* alone. It was just her and the spider that was roaming the halls and rooms. And now that she'd had a good

 94

close-up look at it, she wasn't sure she could face it again, let alone defeat it and save Travis, Rachel, and Mark Dillman.

The words of Captain Duke Ross of the Mars Expeditionary Force suddenly came to mind. *Fear is not the enemy. Not acting in the face of fear is. Now get moving, trooper. Earth depends on you!*

"I don't know about Earth," she said, "but I sure do know that Travis, Rachel, and Mark Dillman are depending on me."

She took a deep breath and thought about her situation. She had the flashlight. She had her vinegar blaster. She did not, however, have a plan. She was back to square one, not sure where the spider had gone or where it had taken Travis.

 95

She kept her back to the wall so that it couldn't surprise her. A quick peek around the corner showed no sign of the spider.

Maybe we've been going about this the wrong way, she thought. *Maybe we should have just looked for Rachel and Mark Dillman right away, instead of chasing the spider.*

Travis, Rachel, and Mark Dillman had to be in the attic. She and Travis had been everywhere else in the house. And didn't spiders like lurking in out-of-the-way places?

She had to get up there. But a direct assault, by herself, was not going to work. All that would accomplish would be to give the spider one more fly for its web.

"Travis," she muttered, "why'd you go and get yourself caught?"

 96

So she'd have to make sure that the spider wasn't up there. That meant luring it out. That meant a decoy. Something to look like a person and attract the monster.

Tara checked the hall again and then made a beeline for Travis's room. First, she needed something that would look like a person's head.

"This ought to do," she said, grabbing one of Travis's soccer balls. "And feet," she said, taking a pair of his sneakers.

She grabbed her robe, her desk lamp, and her skateboard from her room. By the time she was done arranging everything, it looked like someone was sitting down in the hallway. The final touch was an old marble from the mason jar on her dresser. She placed it just

slightly under one of the back wheels. Once it was knocked away, the skateboard would roll down the hallway while the spider (hopefully) chased it.

There was a heavy thud from the attic. Something was moving around above her. It

 98

had to be the spider. It was beginning to move again. Was it wrapping Travis up in webs and going to come look for her?

The spider continued to walk around the attic. It sounded like it was dragging something.

"Come on," she whispered. "Come down here and show yourself."

Tara felt sick. What if they'd waited too long? What if she was too late? What if Mom and Dad came home and it got them, too?

The tube of toothpaste was still where Travis had dropped it. She picked it up and took it into the linen closet with her.

She knelt there, in the dark. There was nowhere else to go, nowhere to run. If it found her . . . She shook her head. *Don't think that*

 99

way, Tara. The flashlight was off, and the door was open a crack. Just enough for her to be able to see it when it emerged from the attic. She opened the toothpaste and squeezed a line out into her palm. She smeared some on her neck and hands as well. If spiders really did not like mint, then it would want no part of her.

She had just finished applying the mint toothpaste when she heard the spider thumping down the attic stairs.

Tara held her breath.

The thumps grew louder. She gritted her teeth tight to keep them from chattering in fear.

It was at the attic door!

Tara clamped her hands over her mouth so that she couldn't scream.

The attic door opened in a slow, lazy arc,

and the massive spider crawled into the hall-way, each leg carefully probing the air and ground. It was being very cautious, almost like it suspected something. It stepped fully into the hallway and stopped. It turned to the right, then turned to the left. It tested the air with its smaller front legs. All its eyes seemed to look everywhere at once, glowing with a deep red, like coals in the middle of the night.

It stalked toward the skateboard. Long legs creeping forward, measuring every step.

Tara's heart pounded. It was so close to the decoy. Any second, it would leap on what it thought was her, and then *WHOOSH!* Down the hall on the skateboard.

But then the spider stopped. It turned in her direction. It stared at the linen closet.

It took one step. Then another. It hunched down and took two quick steps.

Tara pressed herself as far back against the closet wall as she could.

It was almost upon her, and then its forward leg jerked back. It reared up and batted the air with several of its forelegs. It shook itself and hopped backward away from the closet.

The peppermint toothpaste must be working!

The spider turned from the closet and leapt at the decoy instead. The marble rolled out from under the wheel, and the skateboard started down the hallway.

And just like Tara had hoped, the spider darted after it.

 102

11

Tara sprang out of the linen closet and rushed to the attic door. She went in and closed it quietly behind her. She still had her vinegar blaster and the flashlight, but she was afraid to turn it on. It was so dark that the glow would definitely be seen, and she needed every second. If the spider were to see the light, it would race back for her. The peppermint might keep it away from her,

103

but if Travis and the others were up here, she couldn't say the same for them.

She climbed the attic steps like a kitten walking on cotton balls. It wasn't until she reached the top of the stairs that she finally turned on the flashlight. Dust particles danced in the beam of light as she scanned the old attic. Ragged cardboard boxes with Mom's handwriting in marker: *baby clothes*, *donate*, *skiing stuff*. An old cabinet covered in a sheet. Mom's sewing mannequin for when she used to tailor dresses. Grandpa's army trunk and Dad's fishing stuff that Mom moved from the basement, to the garage, to the shed, and to here, its final resting place.

"Travis?" she called out quietly. "Rachel? Mark? Anybody up here?"

She took a few more steps and then stopped dead in her tracks. The flashlight almost fell from her grip.

A massive spiderweb had been spun into the far corner. The thick strands glittered in the light, stretching from the ceiling rafters to the floor to the walls. It was huge, and in the center of it Travis, Rachel, and Mark Dillman were held fast by the sticky webs. As soon as they saw Tara, they started to wriggle and squirm. They tried to call out to her, but the webs covering their mouths made everything an indistinguishable murmur.

Tara moved closer, sidestepping the open pizza box that the spider had snatched.

Something else was in the web, tucked up in the highest corner, under the eaves. She

 105

aimed the flashlight beam directly at it.

It was round and off-white. Parts of it pushed out from the inside, rippling and pulsing. Every few seconds, several darker shapes the size of her hand cast shadows against the outer wall. *Oh no!* It was an egg sac. A *spider* egg sac . . . and there must have been hundreds of baby spiders inside it!

Travis mumbled something and tried to pull free. Tara backed away from the sac. She had to hurry. She had no idea how long it would be before Mama returned to the attic for her babies, or when those babies would hatch. Either of those things could happen at any moment.

"I'm here, Travis," she said. "Hold on!"

She gave the Super Sprayer a few good

pumps and then let the web have it, pumping and spraying as fast as she could. The vinegar did its job and ate through the webs. Travis, Rachel, and Mark Dillman fell to the attic floor.

That noise is sure to bring Mama Spider back on the double, Tara thought.

"I thought I was a goner!" Travis said, pulling long, sticky strands of web from his hair.

"Gross," said Rachel. Her ponytail was plastered to the back of her neck. "I feel sick."

"It's not over yet," Tara said. She tossed the blaster to Travis. "She's coming."

"Who's coming?" squeaked Mark Dillman. His Pizza Mario delivery hat was still stuck in the cobwebs. "You don't mean—"

 108

"Mama," Tara said, pointing her flashlight at the web.

Everyone took a step backward as the baby arachnids inside the egg sac pushed and poked at the thin walls.

Tara quickly wrestled her mother's sewing mannequin down the steps. She had just wedged it between the door handle and the first step when something hit the door so hard, it jolted the whole thing from hinges to frame.

It banged again. And again. But the mannequin held. The spider threw itself at the door in a desperate attempt to get to the attic. It drummed its legs against the door in a furious tantrum.

Tara kept the light on the stairs while

Travis held the Super Sprayer. They'd only have one chance if she were to burst through.

And then the pounding stopped.

"Where did it go?" Rachel asked. "And what are we going to do?"

"Maybe it gave up," said Mark Dillman. "We could make a run for it, right?"

"That's precisely what it wants us to think," whispered Travis. "It wants us to come out."

"Oh man," said Mark Dillman. "We're trapped!"

"Maybe not," Tara said. "Maybe we can get a message out." She nodded toward the attic window.

"Guys?" Rachel said, looking at the web. "I'm not sure we have enough time for that!"

The egg sac jostled and expanded, and

then, with a loud tearing sound, it split open, spilling hundreds of softball-sized, eight-legged babies onto the attic floor.

Rachel screamed, Mark Dillman fainted, and Tara and Travis turned to face the wave of scampering spiders.

12

Tara and Travis stood between the swarm of hatchlings and Rachel and Mark Dillman.

Just as Travis was about to spray the baby spiders with vinegar, they shifted course. The spiders weren't headed for them; they were after the pizza. They swarmed the box, climbing and crawling over one another to get to the slices, carrying away bits of pepperoni and stretches of dough and cheese.

"They're hungry," Tara said.

"Spiders eat pizza?" Travis asked. "Spiders do *not* eat pizza."

"Spiders don't normally write messages, either," Tara said. "I'm beginning to think that—"

CRACK! Glass shattered behind them. They whipped around and watched in horror as the first couple of long, hairy legs pulled the attic window the rest of the way open and the eight angry eyes of Mama Spider glowered down at them.

She saw her spiders. She saw Travis's Super Sprayer full of vinegar. She let out a loud, whistling hiss and clambered across the attic ceiling.

113

Travis raised the blaster and fired, but she was too quick. She dropped into the attic just as the first vinegar blast hit where she'd been only a second ago.

Tara grabbed a nearby fishing pole and swung, but Mama Spider shot a glob of webs from her spinnerets and ripped the rod from Tara's grasp.

Mark Dillman opened his eyes, saw the giant spider raised up on six of its legs, front legs poised to strike, and fainted back to the floor.

Rachel ran for the steps, but Mama Spider planted one leg against Grandpa's old army trunk and pushed it across the floor. Rachel fell over it with a loud "Oof!" that knocked the wind out of her.

Travis stepped back and aimed at the mass of spider babies busily chowing down on what was left of the pizza.

"DON'T EAT US!" screamed Mama Spider.

She sprang forward and landed in front of Travis, blocking his shot.

Travis nearly dropped his Super Sprayer. "Did you—" He tuned to Tara. "Did she just—"

The giant spider took a couple of steps backward, away from Travis and toward her babies. All eyes were on him.

"DON'T. EAT. US," she said in a very scratchy voice.

 115

13

"Travis," said Tara, unable to believe what she was hearing. "Don't move. I think . . ." Tara paused. "I think she's just trying to protect her babies. At least that's what it looks like. All this time she was only trying to keep them safe."

Tara and Travis watched as the babies surged forward, climbing up Mama Spider's many legs and onto her back, where they found their own spot to nestle. Mama's entire body was a mass of wriggling baby spiders.

"If that's the case," he said, "why was she hunting us? Why did she bring Rachel and Mark Dillman up here? Why grab me and put me in her web? Why stop us from warning Sheriff Macklin?"

Mama Spider pointed one of her legs at the vinegar-filled Super Sprayer. She held up another leg, bandaged with her own webbing from when Travis had kicked the basement door closed on it.

"PEOPLE. HURT. SPIDERS," she said.

"Oh, um . . . sorry?" said Travis.

"She definitely could have hurt us if she'd wanted to," said Tara, thinking back to when it had pounced on Travis, twice. "Maybe she

 117

wanted to make sure no one found her babies before they hatched."

"NEEDED. QUIET. PLACE," said Mama Spider. "SAFE. PLACE. DARK. PLACE."

"See?" said Rachel, climbing to her feet. "'They're more afraid of you—'"

"'Than you are of them,'" Travis finished, rolling his eyes.

Baby spiders took turns leaping from Mama Spider's back on the ends of thin strands of web.

"Wheeeeeeeeeeee!" they said in little high-pitched voices before crawling back up to do it again.

"They're kind of cute," said Rachel. "As far as spiders go."

"Okay, so maybe this was all a big mis-understanding?" Travis wondered.

"And maybe we jumped to conclusions," said Tara. "But . . . what are we going to do now? If Mom and Dad—"

"Rachel?" called Dad from the bottom of the main staircase. "Tara? Travis? Where is everyone?"

"Why does the house smell like vinegar?" Mom asked. "And what happened to the power?"

"They're home!" Tara said.

"We're upstairs!" Rachel called. "Just playing . . . hide-and-go-seek!"

"Yeah, um, be down in a minute!" said Travis.

Footsteps sounded outside the attic door, and then someone tried the doorknob.

"Hello? You guys up here?" Mom asked.

The mannequin was still jammed under the knob.

Rachel shook Mark Dillman awake and helped him to his feet.

"I had the strangest dream," he said. "There was this giant spider, and I was in its web. . . ."

"Oh yeah, one second, Mom!" Tara called. "Travis, get the door." She spun back around toward the giant spider. "You have to—"

But the spider was gone. All that was left was a message written in webs:

BE NISE TO SPIDERZ OR ELSE

Tara ran to the attic window just in time to see a large, dark shape scurry behind the garage.

The spider and her babies were gone.

Almost all her babies.

As Rachel, Mark Dillman, Tara, and Travis left the attic, one little set of red eyes watched them from a beam above the door.

And it wouldn't be long before that little set of eyes grew to be a very large set of eyes . . . and legs . . . and fangs.

And so another twisted tale of
Wolver Hollow comes to a close.
You have many questions, no
doubt. Where did the giant spider
come from in the first place?
Where did it go? What about all
those babies? What happened
to the spider in the attic?
Well, no one is quite sure where
she came from, but I can tell you
where she and her babies went.
Three words: NORTHERN PINES RAILROAD.
They took to the trains
leaving town, eager to see
the world, eager to see other
small towns, other attics and
basements. Maybe even attics
and basements like yours.

They made homes in dark
basements and dusty attics all
across the country, and there
they sit, large, and hairy, and
hungry . . . waiting and watching,
with eight red, beady eyes
to make sure that people:

BE NISE TO SPIDERZ.

Acknowledgments

I want to thank my wife, best friend, writing partner, fellow adventurer, and the keeper of my heart, Jess Rinker, for cheering me on, loving my crazy imagination, and for brainstorming with me. We've seen some pretty big spiders together, in our travels (and our house, yikes!), but we always release them into the garden—even the black widow I caught.

Thank you to my always awesome and amazing agent, Jennifer Soloway. I am proud to have you in my corner and thankful for all the hard work you do. I'm so honored to be your author and can't thank you enough! As always, these books would not be what

 125

they are without the superpowered editor extraordinaire Karen Nagel. Wow. You, ma'am, are a rock star! I also need to thank the entire Aladdin team (because it truly takes a team to produce a book)—from layout and design, to the art team, to copyedits, to marketing and sales, and anyone I may have missed—thank you all!

Teo—dude! You crushed it again! Your illustrations are so spot on that I am just in awe. Thank you, sir.

I'm always thankful, and proud of, our children: Shane, Zach, Logan, Ainsley, Sawyer, and Braeden, and our sweet puppies, Pepper and Odin. Love and hugs to all of you.

Shout-out to the Vermont College of

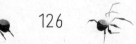

126

Fine Arts (VCFA), and my mentors, Lisa Jahn-Clough, Sharon Darrow, Kathi Appelt, Amy King, and Tom Birdseye.

And finally, thank YOU, readers, for picking up this book, and to the parents, librarians, and teachers who put books like this in the hands of young readers—thank you so much.

Finally, I'd like to encourage everyone to consider not crushing scary-looking spiders when you see them. They're really not a threat, and they do a tremendous amount of good. They don't want to hurt you, or bother you. They really want nothing to do with you. Spiders are amazing creatures. So, if you see a spider that makes your skin crawl, or your heart skip a beat . . . take a second to

remember that it's just as scared of you as you are of it. Leave it alone if you can be so bold, or, if you absolutely have to, find a jar and carefully move it to your yard or garden. Be a friend of spiders. ☺